# WE LOST OUR HOUSE

# 
WE LOST OUR HOUSE

TERESITA BARTOLOME

ReadersMagnet, LLC

2

"Hi, Teresa. Would you like
to play?", asked Anne

"No, not today," answered
Teresa in a sad voice.

"What is happening?" asked
Anne. There's a truck that
says "M-O-V-E-R-S."

"My Dad lost his job. He said we
can't pay for the house anymore so
we have to move out," said Teresa.

"Oh, no! Where are you
moving?" asked Anne.

"My Mom said we'll stay at my
cousins' house temporarily"
answered Teresa. "It is far away."

"What's temporarily?" asked Anne.

"I don't know," said Teresa,
"We can't play Tea Party
and Dress-Up anymore."

MOVERS
5

"Oh. Look they're taking
my piano away now" said
Teresa in a very sad voice.

"But I thought they are helping
you move," said Anne as she
put her arm around Teresa.

"My Mom said we can only bring
small stuff and no furniture.
She said we have to sell most
of our things. See the red pick-
up truck? Those are our things.
That's my Uncle Byron helping
my Dad," explained Teresa.

"Would you like to sit down and talk to Margie?" suggested Anne as she sat on the grass while Teresa crouched. "I feel like crying. My eyes and my chest hurt," said Teresa looking so sad.

"Remember when my cat Iggy
got run-over and he died? That's
how I feel right now," said Teresa,
wiping her tears with her hand.

"I am so sorry," said Anne
her eyes smarting, too.

"Well… I have to go home now. Oh, I forgot it's not our house anymore." said Teresa trying to control her tears. "Teresa, wait!" called Anne.

"Here, you can have Margie.
She always listens when you
talk to her", offered Anne.

"But she is your favorite doll,"
said Teresa feeling a little better.

"It's okay. I don't want you
to be sad. Please don't cry
anymore," said Anne.

"Thank you I will take good care
of Margie. Goodbye, Anne."

"Goodbye, Teresa."

"Teresa, we have to go now.
We'll stop by the store to get
ice cream for everyone." Later
on we'll watch a movie. "Would
you like that?" said Mom as she
hugged Teresa. "Anne's mother
baked a lot of chocolate cookies
for us. That was nice of her. We'll
share them with your cousins."

"Can my cousins, and Auntie Fey
and Uncle Byron come too?"

"Of course", said Mom. Dad
held Teresa in his arms. Teresa
hugged Margie. Then, they
gave the house one last look.

"I love you, Mom. I love you Dad!" said Teresa. "We love you, Teresa. Let's go," said Mom and Dad together.

10620 Treena Street, Suite 230
San Diego, California,
CA 92131 USA
www.readersmagnet.com
1.619.354.2643
Copyright 2020 All Rights Reserved

CPSIA information can be obtained
at www.ICGtesting.com
Printed in the USA
BVHW011548200223
658846BV00021B/648